BUGS BUNNY,™

By Fern G. Brown
Illustrated by Darrell Baker

D0506920

A GOLDEN BOOK • NEW YORK

Western Publishing Company, Inc., Racine, Wisconsin 53404

Western Publishing Company, Inc., offers a wide variety of children's videos, tapes, and games.
For information, write to:
Western Publishing Company, Inc.
1220 Mound Avenue
Racine, WI 53404

"Hey, Porky! Petunia!" Bugs Bunny called excitedly to his friends one summer day. He waved a copy of the *Cotton Tale News* at them. "Did you hear about the writing contest?"

Porky shook his head. "I haven't heard of any contest," he said.

"What contest?" asked Petunia.

"This one!" said Bugs. "The subject is 'My Camping Trip.' Whoever writes the best true camping story wins a backpack—and the winning story will be printed in the newspaper!"

"But we'd have to go camping first," said Petunia, "and we'd need to buy all sorts of equipment."

Bugs grew even more excited. "I've got an idea: Let's rough it! Let's go camping in the wilderness like pioneers! We'll do things the pioneers did— paddle a canoe, cook over an open fire, sing under the stars. I'll write a great story—'Bugs Bunny, Pioneer.' I'm sure to win!" he said smugly.

Porky whispered to Petunia, "Let's go with him. We could enter the contest, too!"

Petunia nodded in agreement. "Maybe *our* stories will get into the newspaper."

Just then, Elmer Fudd drove up. "Hi, folks. How do you like my new van? It's got a sink, table, beds. I'm going camping, and I want to be weally comfy."

Petunia peeked inside the van. "It even has a TV!" she exclaimed.

"How about coming along?" Elmer suggested. "It'll be lots of fun!"

"Wonderful!" said Porky and Petunia.

"Hold it, doc!" Bugs said, blocking the doorway. "I can't win the contest this way. Did the famous pioneers Lewis and Clark ride in a fancy van? No way! They paddled up the river in a *canoe!*"

Reluctantly Petunia said, "Thanks, anyway, Elmer. We're going to rough it with Bugs in the wilderness."

Elmer was disappointed. "What did that wascally wabbit talk you into?"

"So long, doc!" said Bugs before Petunia could reply. "See you on the trail!"

It took a couple of days for Porky and Petunia to get everything ready for the trip.

Bugs made lists of things to take and things to leave behind. He was too busy planning things to do any work.

Finally, Bugs and Porky and Petunia set off in their canoe. Bugs was too busy being a pioneer to paddle but not too busy to give orders to Petunia and Porky. "Stroke! Stroke!" he commanded. "You'll have to go faster if we're going to find a campsite before dark."

"It's hot!" Porky complained, wiping his forehead.

"My shoulder hurts," said Petunia.

Soon they came to a stretch of shallow, rocky rapids. "Everybody out," said Bugs. "It's too hard to paddle here. Carry the canoe across to the other side of the rapids."

"Oh, dear, this canoe is heavy!" Porky cried.

On the other side of the rapids, they got back into
the canoe, and after more paddling, they came to a
sandy clearing on the shore. "This is a perfect spot
for our camp. Beach the boat," Bugs said.

Petunia and Porky dragged the boat onto the beach. "Time to put up the tent," Bugs ordered.

"Wow!" said Porky after he and Petunia put up the tent. "I'm tired. How did the pioneers survive all this work?"

"They were tough—like *us*," Bugs explained.

"Now, like pioneers, we'll have to hunt for food,"
said Bugs. "I brought some carrots, and I see some
wild onions back in that field. Why don't you two
pick them? Then we can have carrot and onion soup."

Bugs leaned against a tree and whittled a stick
while Porky and Petunia picked the onions, made a
fire, chopped the carrots, and cooked the soup. "How
I love the rugged life!" Bugs sighed happily.

The soup was delicious. Bugs, of course, took the biggest share. He patted his stomach. "Mmmm— that was yummy! After you two clear up, let's sit by the fire and relax. I'll play my guitar, and we'll sing under the stars."

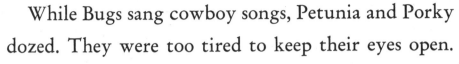

While Bugs sang cowboy songs, Petunia and Porky dozed. They were too tired to keep their eyes open.

One by one, the stars disappeared. Then, suddenly, lightning zigzagged across the dark sky, and thunder rumbled fiercely. "A storm's coming! Get inside the tent!" shouted Bugs, leading the way.

The three campers raced into the tent. The wind blew so hard that the tree branches touched the ground! The earth fairly shook! Rain came down in torrents! A mighty gust of wind tore through the tent, and the tent collapsed!

"Save the canoe!" yelled Bugs as he disappeared into a warm, dry rabbit hole.

The gigantic waves were starting to pull the canoe into the river, but Porky and Petunia caught it just in time. They huddled all night beneath the over-turned canoe to keep dry.

The next morning, the sun was shining. Bugs hopped out of his cozy rabbit hole, stretched his ears, and looked around. "Being a pioneer is fun!" he said. "What are you two whispering about?"

"You!" said Petunia. "You slept nice and warm, but we're cold and tired."

"The canoe has a big hole in it, and we'll have to hike home," Porky said.

"Well, pack the tent and start hiking!" Bugs ordered.

"You've been boss for long enough," decided Petunia. "From now on, we'll give the orders. *You're* going to carry the tent!"

As they started down the road, Bugs groaned. "Hey, doc, this tent is awfully heavy!"

Porky and Petunia smiled at each other.

They hiked for hours, and Bugs never stopped complaining. "Oh, my aching feet!" he moaned. "How much farther do we have to go?"

"Oh, only about ten miles," replied Porky cheerfully, as he and Petunia led the way.

Just then, Elmer drove up in his van. "Boy, are we glad to see you!" said Petunia.

"Hi!" said Elmer. "Did you get caught in the wain? I kept dwy in my van."

"We sure *did* get caught in the rain," Porky answered. "And we're tired of walking. Can we ride home with you?"

"You bet!" Elmer opened the door, and Porky and Petunia hopped in. "Coming, Bugs?" Elmer called.

Before Bugs could answer, Porky asked, "Would Lewis and Clark ride in a van if they were only ten miles from home?"

Bugs gulped as Porky quickly shut the van door. "Thanks, anyway, doc," he said to Elmer. "I'm going to walk."

So Bugs walked and walked and walked. When he was too tired to walk, he *crawled* the last half mile.

It's not all that bad, Bugsy, old boy, he told himself. *You're seeing the country up close—like a real pioneer—and it'll make one humdinger of a story for the contest!*